Diary of Baby a Wombat

written by
Jackie French

illustrated by
Bruce Whatley

HarperCollins *Children's Books*

First published in hardback in Australia by HarperCollins Publishers Pty Ltd in 2009
First published in paperback in Great Britain by HarperCollins Children's Books in 2010

10 9 8 7 6 5 4 3 2 1

ISBN: 978-0-00-735175-6

HarperCollins Children's Books is a division of HarperCollins Publishers Ltd.

Text copyright © Jackie French 2009
Illustrations copyright © Farmhouse Illustration Company Pty Limited 2009

Visit our website at: www.harpercollins.co.uk

Bruce Whatley used acrylic paints on watercolour paper to create the illustrations for this book.

Printed and bound in China

Monday

Early morning: slept.

Slept.

Late morning; slept.

BORED...

Bounced.

Mum decided
It was time to PLAY...

OUTSIDE!

Smelled the flowers.

Ate the flowers.

Flowers are
YUMMMMM...

Another smell...?

It smells like me!

Here it is!

Played with my friend.

I won!

Tuesday

Early morning: slept.

Slept.

Late morning: played.

Afternoon: slept.

Wednesday

Morning: woke up.

BORED...

Mum says we need a new hole. A BIGGER one!

Dug a new hole for all of us.

Afternoon: Scratched.

A lot.

Thursday

Morning: Mum says new hole is too small.

Afternoon: Hunted for **another** new hole.

Will we **ever** find a hole BIG enough for Mum and me?

Friday

Morning:

Found a GIANT hole!

Afternoon:

Told Mum about hole!

Mum said, 'Go to sleep.'

NOT... tired...

Saturday

Morning:

Who stole our hole?

Mum says never mind.

We'll dig the BEST hole EVER!

I wonder
what we'll find up here?

We've found a hole!

The most ENORMOUS hole!

A hole for me ... and my mum.

Sunday

Morning: slept.